3 1994 01319 5901

SANTA ANA PUBLIC LIBRARY
NEWHOPE BRANCH

D1005990

NOTSO HOTSO

ANNE FINE

Notso Hotso

Pictures by Tony Ross

J FICTION FINE, A.
Fine, Anne
Notso hotso

$15.00
NEWHOPE   31994013195901

Farrar, Straus and Giroux

New York

Text copyright © 2001 by Anne Fine
Pictures copyright © 2001 by Tony Ross
All rights reserved
Distributed in Canada by Douglas & McIntyre Ltd.
Printed in the United States of America
First published in Great Britain by Hamish Hamilton Ltd., 2001
First American edition, 2006
1 3 5 7 9 10 8 6 4 2

www.fsgkidsbooks.com

Library of Congress Cataloging-in-Publication Data
Fine, Anne.
    Notso hotso / Anne Fine ; pictures by Tony Ross.— 1st American ed.
      p.   cm.
    Summary: Anthony, a neglected pet dog, develops an irritating skin
condition and has most of his hair shaved off, which embarrasses him
greatly until he realizes he now looks like a lion and can frighten other
animals and people.
    ISBN-13: 978-0-374-35550-0
    ISBN-10: 0-374-35550-9
    1. Dogs—Juvenile fiction.   [1. Dogs—Fiction.   2. Skin—Diseases—
Fiction.   3. Self-esteem—Fiction.]   I. Ross, Tony, ill.   II. Title.

PZ10.3.F493No 2006
[Fic]—dc22

                                                            2004056282

NOTSO HOTSO

1: HOW THE HORROR BEGAN

So suddenly one morning I'm like, *Scratch-scratch! Scratch-scratch!* and can't stop. It's disgusting.

Everyone else thinks so too.

"Anthony, stop doing that."

"Would someone please put that pest-ridden dog out?"

"Knock it *off*, Anthony!"

Hey! Notso hotso!

Especially for someone like me. I'm not fussy, exactly. (Personally, I'd call it fastidious, though I know one or two have rather harshly used the word

prissy.) But I'm not one of those mucky
I'm-a-Mutt-and-I'll-Scratch-If-I-Like

pups. I suppose I just think the world's a nicer place for all of us if everyone tries to keep their smells and messes and nasty little personal habits quietly to themselves.

Call me a fussbudget if you will, but I just like to help keep things nice.

And skin problems aren't nice. As fellow sufferers will know, skin problems aren't something you can forget for the morning. They drive you mad, especially the itchy ones. First you think, if you just scratch this tiny bit here . . .

Then you think, if you just have a little go at that itsy-bitsy patch there . . .

And then you think, now you've started anyway, you might as well scratch sideways on this part here . . .

And before you know where you are, every single bit of you is aflame.

I'm not exaggerating. I mean, AFLAME.

And no one sympathizes. They just think you're being annoying.

"Anthony, if you don't stop that

dreadful scratching, I'll put you outside again, even though it's raining."

"Anthony! Stop that! Now!"

Talk about a dog's life. If it hadn't been for Moira next door, I might have scratched myself to pieces.

"What's wrong with your dog?"

As if that Joshua would take his eyes off his game for a moment to glance at his own pet. "Nothing."

"Yes there is, Joshua. He's dropping weird flakes all over your carpet."

I'm not even going to *tell* you about the next bit. It's just too horrible. Suffice it to say that it involved an argument about whether or not that stuff all over the rug was actually bits of dead dog skin. And then we had to wait while Moira went home to borrow her granny's magnifying glass. And then I had to put up with the two of them endlessly prodding and patting me.

"Ugh! Yuck! That is some sick stuff floating off his back!"

"Gruesome! You ought to tell your mum."

"Mum? She'd throw up if she saw this!"

Nice, eh? I expect he's forgotten some of his own rather disgusting habits. And as for Moira, well, I've seen her often enough, sitting with her back to the house, doing things to her nose she wouldn't do in front of anyone except me, and possibly Belinda, her pet hamster.

At least the two of them did something useful when my Humiliation Hour was up. They told Her Ladyship.

"Mu-*um*! There's something wrong with Anthony."

"Yes, Mrs. Tanner. Come and look at this. It's *horrible*!"

So Mrs. Neglectful finally ambles to the doorway, carelessly dropping cheese from the grater she's holding. (One small bright spot in the day for me.)

"What sort of wrong?"

"His skin's all coming off."

"Coming off?"

"Yes. In horrible, yucky, revolting little flakes."

(Well, thank *you*, Joshua. And don't expect any company or sympathy next time you get the chicken pox.)

"Yes, Mrs. Tanner!" chimes in Moira. "He's all rashy red underneath. And bits of him have gone gooey."

(Fine, Moira. Just don't sit waiting for me to waste any more of my time fetching sticks to amuse you next time you're stuck at home with the measles.)

The Kitchen Queen strolls over. I'm hoping she at least has the sense to put the grater down before she touches me. And then wash her hands thoroughly. After all, as I said, I wouldn't call myself *fussy*. But I do like the leftovers that get scraped into my bowl to be reasonably wholesome.

Touching me, nothing! Mrs. What?–

In-My-House? draws back. "Ugh! That is *horrible*. That is *repellent*."

Well, thank you very much. Is there anyone out there, reading this, who's been wanting a crowd of insensitive people?

Because I've got a load here.

A whole *set*.

2: GETTING WORSE AND WORSE

Personally, I'd have thought it was an emergency. But not her. Not Lady Laid-back.

"Is it an emergency?" the vet's assistant asks over the phone.

"No," she says. (Just like that: "No.")

And she settles for an afternoon appointment on Thursday.

However, get this. Later that day, when Mr. Whoops-Sorry-Forgot-to-Pick-Up-the-Dog-Food-Again strolls in from work, she orders him straight back out to buy a pack of vacuum cleaner bags. "No, you *can't* leave it till later,"

she tells him when he starts grumbling. "Not with flakes of dog skin all over. This is an *emergency*."

Not the most sensitive bunch. And don't think I'm making it up when I tell you I haven't been shooed out of the house quite so forcefully or so often since that toddler with the allergies was visiting last Easter.

I made the most of it—even turned into a bit of a sun worshipper on the sly, after I'd walked past Lady Vain's pile of beauty magazines on her bedroom floor and seen an article that claimed that—sensibly handled—ultraviolet light can work wonders with what they tactfully call "iffy" skin.

Though that great snoring slug-

colored heap on Next-door's wall did
turn a bit brutal when I stretched out to

offer my poor itching flanks to the Great Eye of Heaven's healing powers.

"Looking a bit 'bare rug,' aren't you, Anthony? Have the family been feeding you Hair-Fall-Out pills?"

"Nice," I said. "Coming from a cat that's as big as a barrel."

"Go gnaw a doorknob, Ant!"

I hate it when that cat calls me "Ant." So I snuck back inside. And got shooed out again. And thought, "Okay, then. It's their fault if I go a-wandering."

And I went down to the park.

I'm not the gang type, on the whole. It's not my scene. I think smell tours are juvenile. When Buster and Hamish and Bella overexcite themselves, their tongues get a bit piggy. And I don't care for the way that, when they're playing Dingoes vs. Jackals, they leave a trail of mashed bushes behind them.

From time to time, I say a word on the subject.

"Could you take a little more care?" I plead. "Some of us have to walk in this park every morning. Please try to leave the place as pleasant as you found it."

They jeer, of course.

"Well, if it isn't Oily Anthony, the park keeper's pal."

"I'm really, really worried!"

"Oh, bite me! Bite me!"

Most days, our Buster's in his I'm-the-Leader-of-the-Pack mood. I pad up. He turns, gives me the ultra-unfriendly Lost-Are-You? stare, and says, "Fall out of your basket, Anthony?"

I roll my eyes. I mean, that sort of sarcasm is so ten minutes ago. (Or even earlier.) "Well, don't you absolutely reek of cool!" I scoff, and wait for his hackles to rise and that stupid little growl that's supposed to mean "Watch it, Mr. Nothing-from-Nowhere," before he invites me to traipse around with them.

But today things are different. He's taking an interest, almost.

"What's wrong with you?"

Hamish joins in. "Yeah. You look weird. Like a bare rug with feet."

(Just what that nasty cat said. *Now* I'm listening.) "What do you mean?"

So Bella explains. "You're missing great patches of fur at the back."

Hamish agrees. "You look *terrible*."

Trust Buster to be a whole lot more unpleasant than necessary. "You told us you were a sheepdog-retriever mix," he crows. "You never admitted you were a one hundred percent molter."

I'm getting worried now—shimmying around to try and get a look at the parts I've been scratching. "It can't be that bad, surely."

"In your dreams!"

"In never-never land!"

"Well, somebody's been putting *something* in your mystery chow."

Up puffs Old Nigel, who's spent the last ten minutes wheezing and staggering across the park toward us at the speed of winter turning to spring.

"My word!" he quavers. He can't take his rheumy eyes off me. "You look even worse than I feel. I reckon you won't last any longer than I will."

Talk about *panic*. I just turned and *fled*.

3: MIRROR, MIRROR, ON THE WALL

So now I'm serious about getting a proper look at my back and sides. Of course, since the flaking began, My Lady House-Proud has kept me right out of her flouncy-wouncy bedroom with the floor-to-ceiling mirror. But it's in there I creep when she's not looking. (I have to be careful. Last time she caught me hanging around the door, she said, "You so much as *step* in here while you're shedding that stuff on the carpets, Anthony, and I will roast you on a spit!" *And* I believed her.)

So slinky was the word. I made it

safely to under the bed. Then out the other side to the mirror.

Oh, horror! Oh, the horror! Imagine sleek and glossy me, twisting my rear end around to take a peek at what was once the perfect hide, and finding . . .

Mange!

In places, my bum was raw. If I had been a carpet, you would have tossed me out without a thought. I was appalled. I take my cod liver oil. I get enough fresh air. I exercise. (In fact, of all the dogs around here, I'm probably the most particular about looking after my health and keeping regular habits.)

It wasn't fair. I looked *shocking*. And if I hadn't been exactly where I was most particularly not supposed to be, I would have raised my head and *howled*.

As it was, I just whimpered.

That's when she walked in. I didn't wait for the rocket I knew was coming. (Something along the lines of "Anthony! Didn't I *warn* you that if you came in here . . . blah-blah-blah—") Tucking my tail between my legs, I slunk toward the door. Lord knows, I'm

no slave to glamour. Ours is a mongrel world, and crossbreeds like myself know only too well that judging by appearances can all too easily lead to—

Hang on a bit! What was this?

Miss Sneak-in-My-Room-and-I'll-Roast-You had thrown herself onto her knees at my side. She had her arms

around my neck, and she was practically in tears herself.

"Oh, Anthony! You poor lamb! You're in *misery*, aren't you? You're actually *whimpering*. Oh, you poor darling."

And suddenly she's on the phone. "No!" she's telling the vet's assistant. "Thursday *won't* do. The poor creature's in agony. I don't care how many people you have waiting. This is an *emergency*, and I'm bringing him *now*."

Next thing I know, I'm standing trembling on the examination table, and Delia Massingpole, B.V.Sc., M.R.C.V.S., is peering at me through a little lens.

"Yes, very nasty. It must itch a lot."

After five years in vet school? This I could tell her for free! But I just stand

there, shedding quietly, while she looks some more.

Then out it comes. I couldn't bring myself to listen to the details, so to this day I'm not quite sure whether she said it was scabies masquerading as mange with a little touch of eczema, or mangy eczema with a faint veneer of scabies, or all three at once. All I know is I tried to keep my head high and ponder inner beauty.

Suddenly Ms. Massingpole is handing over a giant tub of gloppy-looking yellow cream. "This should do the trick."

Lady It's - an - Emergency - When - I - Say-So unscrews the lid and sniffs. "It doesn't smell very nice."

Hel-*lo*! I'm thinking. The stuff's not supposed to go in your bath. Or on your face. It's supposed to go on my bottom. And just so long as it does the trick, like Vet Massingpole thinks, things are peachy by me.

Miss Shed-on-My-Rugs-and-I'll-Kill-

You is still looking dubious. "How am I supposed to rub it on him?"

I'll sit still, I am promising silently. I will sit *still*.

But that's not what she's worrying about. "This stuff's so tacky, I'll never get it out from under my fingernails."

Oh, dear me! I hope you know I'm practically falling off the table here, from sheer anxiety and grief on her behalf. Good heavens! Maybe she'd better take me home straightaway and let me scratch myself *bald*, rather than risk getting even a dab of icky, nasty-smelling yellow stuff under one of her perfect Sugar Frost talons.

"I've got an idea," said First-in-Command Massingpole. "We'll shave him."

Well, whose side is *she* on?

I stare.

And so does Mrs. T. "Shave him?"

"Yes. It's a much better idea." (I'm

frozen with horror. She's plugging in the razor.) "We'll shave the fur that's left. That way, the cream will rub in better. The problem will go away faster. And all his fur will grow back soon enough."

Oh, sure! A peachy plan!

For *her*.

I turn my head to the lady who first picked me out from behind bars; who first decided I would be an asset to her family; who bought me my first-ever real dog bed and my bright red plastic bowl; who came down *fifteen times* on my first night to comfort and reassure me.

She loves me. I *know* it.

But guess what the weaselly traitor said to Butcher Massingpole?

"Brilliant. Let's do it!"

4: TALK ABOUT *TOUGH*

They were pitiless, those ladies. I don't think I've ever put up such a struggle, and I can't remember ever losing a fight so fast.

Talk about *tough*. Milady Massingpole wielded the shaver like someone in a horror film you're too young to watch, and, get this, threatened me with *anesthesia* if I kept wriggling!

And the Hand-Cream Queen pinned me down with her elbows. (I take as much care of my paws as the next pup, but really, these perfect fingernail worries of hers are truly getting out of hand.)

Bzzzz.

Bzzzz.

Bzzzzzzzzzzz.

BZZZZZZZZZ.

I certainly hope nobody ever does anything halfway as brutal to you. When they'd finished, the floor looked like a hairdresser's, the day girls with shiny skulls come back into fashion.

And I was *naked*. My skin looked like plucked chicken.

They broke off for a teensy-weensy discussion about where to stop.

"Are you going to shave all the way down his tail?"

"Yes, I'll just leave the tuft at the very end."

"What about his head?"

Cruella Massingpole inspects my head for more of whatever it is that has landed me in her den of shame. "He's clear from the neck up. So let's

leave the head and see how he goes."

See how he *goes*? Perhaps she means, see over which cliff he throws himself. Or see how, with all the stuffing knocked out of him, he takes to his dog bed and pines to death quietly.

See how he goes, indeed! He goes exactly how you'd expect him to go.

Pretty darn quick!

I wasn't going to let those nosy Nellies in the waiting room get an eyeful of this spring's new fake-o-la oven-ready retriever look. No, sirree! The minute she'd finished rubbing that disgusting yellow glop all over my poor shaven body and lifted me down from the table, I shot off.

Taking the Maniac Massingpole utterly by surprise, I spun around and dashed between her legs, and out the back way, past all her shelves of fancy He-Won't-Even-Notice-This-Needle-Going-into-Him syringes (Dream on! We're not all half dead like Old Nigel), past lines of cages stuffed with scowling cats busy licking their stitches, and out the back door to the parking lot.

And there I waited, lurking behind a large CUSTOMERS ONLY sign, in case anyone saw me.

Finally, out she comes, all smiles and wheedling. "Anthony! Anthoneeee!"

She thinks I'm *stupid*?

I give her a growl. Unlock the car! it means. Open the door! Let me in, out of sight, *quick*!

"Oh, *there* you are, hon!" She's smiling at me. Mrs. Betrayal has the nerve to *smile*. "It's all right, darling. You're safe now. That nasty vet lady has finished upsetting you."

I see. She thinks my memory's been shaved off too. Well, I don't think so! I

seem to remember *two* people bending over me, pinning me down.

Working as a *team*.

(And don't think this mutt will be hurrying back for his boosters.)

All the way home, I'm planning my next smart move. If she thinks I'm going to pad up the garden path with my head held high, she is crazy. For one thing, the gossip will get around this neighborhood like news in a rabbit warren . . .

I can see it now. Straight from the headlines of *The Daily Bunny*:

HUGE, PLUCKED, FOUR-LEGGED CHICKEN SIGHTED ON JUNIPER AVENUE

In this issue:
Are We in Danger?
And Our Science Man Asks:
"Has Genetic Meddling Gone Too Far?"
See pages 2, 3, 4, 14 & 16.
Plus!
Favorite chicken-leg recipes!
Snatched photos in our
special pull-out supplement.
Completely FREE!

No, thanks. I'll nip up the side of the house under cover of the lilacs, hide in the knapsack under the bed in the spare room, and wait till I grow out.

I'm ready. Like a highly trained member of some crack army team, I have my head down but I'm poised to fly. She

flaps about a bit as usual, shoveling lip-
sticks back in her cosmetics collection in
the glove compartment, and picking bits
of used tissue off the floor.

And then she gets out, slams her
door, and comes around the back to
open mine.

I didn't mean to shove her into the
gillyflowers. That really wasn't part of
the plan. It's just that, as we professionals
so often say:

HE WHO DARES, WINS

And only a greyhound could have
come after me. I shot down that side en-
trance so fast, my slipstream very nearly
set fire to the trash can. I had my eye on
cornering at Formula One speeds, jam-

ming myself out of sight between the shed and the wall, and then, when she opened the back door and started with her pathetic greasy wheedling —"Anthony! Oh, Anthoneeeeeeee!"— hurling myself past her so fast I'd look blurry.

Who's there to ruin the Great Plan? What's the first thing I see as I come around the corner?

Why, Next-door's cat, of course, idling its life away as usual in one of the sunny spots on our wall.

That's *it*, I'm thinking. *Doomed.* The

whisper will get down the street so fast that even before Miss I'll-Just-Put-the-Kettle-On-before-I-Call-Anthony bothers to stroll to the back door, that cat'll be selling tickets:

Come and Laugh at Ant!
Price: A carton of cream
(or a bit of cooked liver)

And what happens?

The weirdest thing. (Maybe a miracle.)

The cat doesn't recognize me.

Does it slap on its usual snooty Oh-Yawn,-It's-That-Wuss-Anthony-Again look?

No, it doesn't. It looks as if someone has shoved a billion volts of electricity up its tail.

Does it arch its back and spit nastily?
No.
Does it hang about sneering?
No, it does not.
It vanishes.
Just like that!

Always good to see the back of that cat, but, really, this was spectacular.

It made up for a lot.

As soon as Her Ladyship had stopped calling "Anthoneee!" I slunk to the door.

(I wasn't going to have her think I was obeying orders after the grievous bodily harm she'd done to me.)

I had a listen. Excellent! She'd gone upstairs to give Joshua some grief for leaving a trail of chips along the hall and up the stairs. I vacuumed my way up after them, and passed his bedroom door while she was still spooning out her motherly lecture.

". . . blah-blah-blah-told you once, must have told you a million times . . . blah-blah-blah—"

Good thing I'd nearly reached the spare room. Already my eyes were glazing over, and boredom was making my legs weak.

But suddenly even the Nagger Queen lost interest in what she was saying. She

broke off. "Oh, never mind," she told him. "Come down and have some tea, and I'll tell you all about this afternoon."

Explain what a hoot it was, I expect she meant. Give you a good laugh. But there was no time to stand around being bitter. She was already backing out, and there was nowhere to vanish

except through the door to her own room.

Abracadabra! I'm gone.

If I was quiet before, now I'm on serious tippy-toes. I know as well as you that anyone who has Yours Truly for a pet can cry "No worries!" when they spot a bit of finger food at rest on the carpet.

So if she was dishing out a scolding to Joshua for the lightest of shrimp-flavored-potato-chip spills, I wouldn't want to be the fellow standing with his head hung low at the moment she notices yellow glop on her nice velvet curtains.

No, I gave the soft furnishings the widest berth. I stayed on tippy-toes. I didn't wag. (No problem there.)

I just prudently removed myself to the other side of the bed.

Beside the mirror.

Aaaargh!

Talk about fright! I nearly died! I don't think I've ever felt my poor heart pound so fast.

Put it this way. You'd guessed already that the vet had ruined your looks, and your social life, and any chance you had of making friends outside of the Ugly Club.

But now you realize that Next-door's cat didn't hurry off because you had problem breath.

Oh, no.

She obviously hightailed it because she saw what I was looking at in Ms. Vanity's mirror.

And that, standing boldly in the bedroom, was a huge lion.

5: CAT TEST

I'm going to speak up for young Moira now. That girl was *sweet*. After she'd finished screaming and all had been explained, she settled down on the patio with Joshua and started to stroke me.

Actually stroke me.

Not the sticky bits, obviously. (Unless she had mange too, that would have been silly.) Just my head and my ruff. But it was soothing. It was comforting. It made me feel less like a freak.

And it was Moira who put the idea in my head.

"Hey, Joshua," she said. "Let's take Anthony for a walk down to the mall and pretend he's a real lion."

Down to the mall, nothing! I hate down to the mall. Overconfident toddlers poking their fingers in your eye. And children the same age as you crooning, "Oooh! What's his name? Can I stroke him? Will he bite me?" Or that old make-you-growler, "Is he a boy or a girl?" (Do I *look* like a girl? Oh, yes, maybe. To someone with their head in a bucket!)

Even the joy of getting away is spoiled, with every shopkeeper making the same old tired joke. "You should get your Anthony to carry everything home for you, Mrs. Tanner."

No. I hate down to the mall.

But that "pretend he's a lion" bit—
that made my ears prick up. First, shake
off the bodyguards. I acted casual—you
know the sort of thing: "I'll just step out
for a moment. Call of nature, you un-
derstand. Back in a minute." They didn't
suspect a thing.

Neither did she. Miss Wasted-Enough-Time-on-You-Already-Today opened the back door with barely a word. (How fast sympathy shrivels.)

And I was out.

Cat test!

I must have done a pretty good job first time around, because the charmer wasn't back on our wall as usual, acting the fur slug. The secret of tracking, of course, is Know Your Enemy. So I thought back to the last time Old Tub o' Lard was in a major snit, and that was after it had come back from one of Stitcher Massingpole's cages.

It spent that whole week in the garden shed, licking its wound.

I take a peek. Yes! Door a fraction

open. Tell Sherlock Holmes he needn't come. Anthony's on the case now.

Squeeze through the fence. (That scraped a bit of glop off both sides. Time to start watching my weight again!)

Then, *creepy-creep-creep. Creepy-creep-creep.*

(I'm loving this. As you have probably guessed, nobody calls me "Scary Anthony." They don't tremble when they see me. And once, when I overheard Bella saying "Frightened of his own water bowl!" I noticed that everyone was looking in my direction.)

I'm ready now. What noise do lions

make? I know they roar. But how does that go exactly? In this house, we don't get to watch much wildlife stuff. She's into cooking and decorating programs. He has the sports channel on until all

hours. And Joshua prefers those cheap and tasteless teenage sitcoms.

I think the last time I saw a lion on television was Christmas Eve.

Yes. In *The Lion King*!

ROOOOAAAAAAAR!!!!!!!!!!

Not bad, for a first shot. And what with my appearing in the doorway suddenly, good enough for that cat. Another trillion volts! The thing shot up like something in a horror film. (We *all* watch those.) Practically hit its head on one of the two-by-four rafters.

Big shock, big noise. Right now, the thing was yowling fit to burst, trapped in its hidey-hole. (Not quite so cozy *now*.)

But I knew if it caught sight of me again, terror might fuel enough of its little brain cells for it to catch on.

Hey! Notso hotso!

So, yes. Good practice. *Excellent* rehearsal.

But time to go now.

Time for the Big Show.

6: FUN-TIME

I found them sniffing trash cans. Honestly! Would you—*could* you— imagine being bored enough to sniff a trash can? Darting from under Miss Forsyth's holly bush across to Mr. Hall's hedge, I made it to the park gates without being seen. And while the three of them were chasing a couple of pudgy squirrels back up their tree—as if, gang, as if!—I slid around the corner the other way.

Into the kiddies' playground.

Hey! Not my fault! Moira's mum says nannies get bees in their panty hose

about things like a spider in the bath. I grant you, seeing a lion staring out at you from behind the baby swings probably sucks big time; but that's no reason to deafen everyone on your way out with your horrible screeching.

The gang came running. (No one likes missing a bit of fun.) But I was thinking this treat was far too good to waste on all of them in one big go, so I slid away between the compost heap and the toolshed, toward the old picnic pavilion.

And that's where I bumped into Old Nigel.

Clearly he'd only been let out to play about a trillion years ago, because he was still only halfway across the fifty yards from his own house. He stopped

for one of his little twenty-minute breaks in between steps. And tried lifting his head. And made an effort to focus.

And then he (sort of) saw me.

And (sort of) stopped.

Dead.

I choose my word carefully here. I don't mean "froze." There's something

alive about "froze." "Froze" gives the idea of alert and ready.

Nigel was just . . . stopped.

I stood and waited. But really, it was about as exciting as watching Granny get ready for bed. So in the end I simply thought, "I'll come back later," and rushed away, into the Quiet Dell.

I don't usually take the shortcut
through here, because there's a NO

DOGS sign. But, hey! Today I'm a lion.

And, strolling through, I cause a bit of a ripple.

"Bertha? Is that a *lion* I see over there?"

"It can't be, Gladys. It must be a speck on your glasses."

"I really do believe it is a lion, dear."

"Well, if you say so. Do you suppose the poor lamb would like a bit of my sandwich?"

I'm standing waiting to hear more—like, the answer is *yes* if it's ham or turkey but *no* if it's apricot jam—when, suddenly, into the dell stroll Buster and Hamish. I *ask* you, what is the point of having a NO DOGS sign if everyone ignores it?

And dangling from Buster's mouth is The Lost Bone.

All right. I freely admit it. Lots of bones get lost. We have lost bones all over. (Somewhere.) But this bone was totally special. It was cooked. And meaty. And it dripped with marrow. And it had been lost for months, since the day Buster buried it because he couldn't deal with it. (He'd been vacuuming up after a party with pizzas and kebabs—I tell you, watch those skewers: they are *dangerous*.) I'll spare you the grisly details. Let's just say that some of those half-eaten desserts left on the floor behind the sofa had *way* too much sherry and coffee brandy in them.

So Buster reeled out in the dark night

to bury his bone, and could hardly remember a thing in the morning.

For just a moment, I forgot the lion
bit.

"Hey!" I said, friendly as a six-

month-old spaniel. "You finally found the old trophy bone!"

Buster's not listening. One look at me, the bone's on the grass, and Buster is running.

And Hamish isn't far behind.

I pick up The Lost Bone. Excellent! More fun on Monday, when I am the only one who knows where to find it. I dig a little hole behind Gladys. (It turns out her sandwich is falafel and anchovy, and therefore definitely not for me.) And then I sashay off around the corner.

Only to bump into Bella.

Where flee turns out to be spelled f-l-i-r-t.

She sees me and starts sweeping the path with her eyelashes.

And guess what she says. "Well, hel-*lo*, Big Boy! Fancy a stroll around the trash cans?"

My turn to flee! I made it back to

the picnic area, where twenty old-timers playing a big boccie ball match scattered.

"Lion! Lion on the loose! Lion!"

"Are you *sure*, Gregory?"

"Lion!"

One of them threw a boccie ball. It kind of rolled up gently between my paws. I tried to roll it back. (Talk about *heavy*. I pushed my hardest and the thing got *nowhere*. These grizzled folk must be a whole lot tougher than they look.)

Not wanting to trash the image, I slid away between the bushes—back into the clearing, where Nigel is still sort of standing there, still sort of *stopped*.

"Nigel?" I said. "Nigel?"

He's staring at me with those sad old sheep's eyes. But nothing more. Not a flicker.

"Come on, Nigel." I gave him the tiniest of nudges. "Take a step."

He rocked a bit dangerously, but nothing else happened.

I went back around the front. He was still staring at me, but he wasn't blinking.

Uh-uh! Notso hotso. I always thought that when there was nothing left to hold you up, you probably fell over. But that's

arthritis for you, I expect. It is a *scourge*.
Nigel often said as much.

He couldn't stay there, could he? No,
of course he couldn't.

And I couldn't carry him.

So I used subterfuge. I stood beside
him and I howled. Pitifully! I howled
like the Lost and the Damned all herded
together. I howled to bring people with
stones for hearts running with stretchers.

And as soon as I heard all the foot-steps getting closer, I nipped out of sight in the bushes.

So then it's instant replay with the adults.

"What's up, old boy? What's all this noise about?"

"Thorn in your paw?"

"Lost one of your puppies?" Closer look. Correction. "Great-great-great-grandpuppies?"

Nigel is saying nothing.

So one of the blokes reaches over to stroke him.

Mistake!

Over he keels.

TIM-*BER*!!!

I won't say the real word, in case we have a few soft-hearted souls out there,

reading this at bedtime. (I like to keep things "family.") Let's just admit Old Nigel was not exactly in peachy form. He wasn't quite himself. His own little personal party was over.

A blessing really. His life had been a burden to him for quite a while. Any responsible owner would have taken him up to Ms. It's-Kinder-and-I-Assure-You-He-Won't-Feel-a-Thing Massingpole the very first time he . . .

Hey! No time for morbid chat! The speciality howling had brought the park keepers running. It was time to go.

Fun over.

There's not much more to tell. The chaos I caused made it into the paper. (I could have done without the word *mangy* appearing quite so often, but, hey! That's the tiger of fame: you can't ride it.) Poor Bella—she was blushing for a while. (We all call her the Lion Queen.) I made a deal with Buster: no respect—no bone. And I doubt if he'll be teasing me so much or so often.

And we all went to Nigel's funeral. (Bit of a "dig and drop," if you want my opinion. It could have been nicer, but there you go, if you're not there to see it, I guess it doesn't really matter.)

And, next day, Hamish left his squeaky bunny outside our gate, so I'd have something to do till the old hairs grow back again, and I can come out without everyone pointing.

"See him? I read about that dog in the paper. It seems what happened *was* . . ."

It's quite a tale, huh?

But, fact is—it's over.